# Mem Fox

# HUNWICK'S EGG

Illustrated by **Pamela Lofts**

HARCOURT, INC.

Orlando   Austin   New York   San Diego   Toronto   London

Printed in Singapore

O nce upon a time, at the edge of a wide
and dusty desert, there lived an old bandicoot.

His name was Hunwick.

One morning Hunwick sat up
and sniffed the wind.

A storm was on its way, and when
it broke, what a storm it was! The
world was tossed inside out and
upside down.

In the evening, when the skies had cleared, there lay, close to Hunwick's burrow, a most curious egg.

"You look lost," Hunwick said.

Hunwick called on his neighbors.
"Whose egg might this be?" he asked.
   None of them knew.
   "I have never seen an egg so beautiful,"
said Emu.
   "It must come from far away," said
Echidna.
   "It needs a home," said Cockatoo.

"Then I will give it one,"
said Hunwick.
      And he took the egg back
to his burrow and bustled
about, making things cozy.

"You'll be safe with me," Hunwick said.
His heart felt light. He was already fond
of the egg and wondered what would happen
when it hatched.

Each evening before he went out to find food,
Hunwick covered the egg with twigs.
As he left he smiled and said, "Now
do behave while I'm away!"
    And then he waved good-bye,
although the egg never waved back.

Neither did it hatch.

One night, when the stars were coming out in
twos and threes, Hunwick was brave enough to
speak his mind. "I'm glad I found you,"
he said, not looking at the egg directly.

The egg made no reply.

Neither did it hatch.

Hunwick and the egg often sat side by side
in the moonlight. Hunwick would tell stories
from his past, exaggerating here and there
from time to time. He also shared his troubles.
The egg listened in respectful silence
but did not say a word.

Neither did it hatch.

At bedtime Hunwick would hold the egg close. "We're together, you and I," he'd say, "and this is our home."

The egg was a good friend to Hunwick.
It listened well. And it was always there.

But Hunwick's neighbors watched, and
worried, and wondered.

"That egg," said Emu. "Will it *ever* hatch?"

"Not now," said Echidna.

"Not ever," said Cockatoo.

"Poor Hunwick," they said together.

But Hunwick wasn't sad. He had guessed long
before that the egg was not an egg at all, but a stone
of perfect shape, and size, and color.
"I don't mind," he said to himself. "I love it as it is."
And he continued to love it with all his heart.
It was his egg. It was his secret.

And it remained his friend forever.

*For Kathy Keech, who loves animals—M. F.*

*For Helen, with love—P. L.*

Text copyright © 2005 by Mem Fox
Illustrations copyright © 2005 by Pamela Lofts

www.HarcourtBooks.com

Library of Congress Cataloging-in-Publication Data
Fox, Mem, 1946–
Hunwick's egg/Mem Fox; illustrated by Pamela Lofts.
p.  cm.
Summary: When a wild storm sends a beautiful egg to Hunwick the
bandicoot's burrow, he decides to give it a home and become its friend.

[1. Eggs—Fiction.  2. Bandicoots—Fiction.  3. Friendship—Fiction.]
I. Lofts, Pamela, ill.  II. Title.
PZ7.F8373Hu 2005
[E]—dc22  2003016385
ISBN 0-15-216318-2

First edition

H G F E D C B A

With special thanks to the Alice Springs Desert Park, Australia, for help
with research on the bilby. The bilby, also known as the rabbit-eared
bandicoot, is an endangered species.

The illustrations in this book were done in watercolor pencil on
Fabriano Cotton watercolor paper.
The display type was created by Judythe Sieck.
The text type was set in Quadraat.
Color separations by Bright Arts Ltd., Hong Kong
Printed and bound by Tien Wah Press, Singapore
This book was printed on totally chlorine-free Stora Enso Matte paper.
Production supervision by Ginger Boyer
Designed by Pamela Lofts and Judythe Sieck